the Gift of an Angel

the Gift of an Angel

is dedicated to Jim
who knows all the reasons why. MR

Marianne Richmond Studios, Inc.
420 N. 5th Street, Suite 840
Minneapolis, MN 55401
www.mariannerichmond.com

ISBN 0-9741465-2-8

Illustrations by Marianne Richmond

Book design by Sara Dare Biscan

Printed in China

Eighth Printing

For every child, there is an angel
hand–chosen in heaven above
and sent on a star to earth below
to protect, to teach, to love.

To _____

From _____

With the golden light of sunrise,

morning dawned upon the earth.

A day composed in heaven

for a baby's blessed birth.

Gentle color erased night's shadows.

Warm breezes nudged the world awake.

Bees and butterflies began to play,

as sunshine kissed the lake.

All things living danced in harmony

to the melody of love

as expectant hearts prepared to greet

their dear child from above.

Amidst all this earthly ardor,

heaven stirred with anticipation

as God tended to the special gift

for His miracle of creation.

Gathering His host of angels,

the Lord considered them one by one.

"I need a volunteer," He said,

"to watch over this daughter or son.

"I've created a child so unique,

yet so needy of guidance and care.

I want to insure that an angel

will for this child be there."

Then a beautiful angel with demeanor

always gentle, always mild,

accepted the Lord's invitation

to be guardian of the child.

Pensively, the angel asked,

"For this family, what can I do?

Aren't the parents you've chosen capable?

Won't they watch this child for you?"

"They will, my angel," said the Lord.

"But they can't be everywhere.

That's why I wish to give to them

my constant loving care.

"Your role in the child's life,

will gently unfold with the days.

You'll be a protector, keeper, friend . . .

and wise teacher of life's ways.

"You'll inspire the child to explore

as only a little child can,

with wide-eyed wonder and innocence,

with impulsive abandon.

"You'll nudge your child to open

the door to where dreams can run free—

a world where the curious spirit

plays with fun and spontaneity.

"A place where a child can play pretend

with pirates, fairies and kings,

living on high seas and in strong castles

orchestrating awesome, imaginative things.

"And you'll lead the child down paths

filled with wonders of everyday—

a pudgy caterpillar, a plump bumblebee,

a butterfly meandering her way.

"You'll bestow on this family the wonder

that lets parents see through

child's eyes, helping them recapture

the innocence and moments of sweet surprise.

"Through you, they'll know heaven's goodness,

gentle peace that comes with love.

Days will be radiant and nights be filled

with quiet harmony from above."

Then the angel teetered on heaven's edge,

peering down on a waiting earth.

For a brief moment all time stood still

just moments before the birth.

"One more thing, dear angel, before you go,"

said the Lord to His chosen one.

"Life is not always laughter and smiles . . .

not all discovery and fun.

"There will be frightening times for sure

when danger stirs alarm.

It's then you must forget all else

and protect this child from harm."

"I understand," the angel said,

"the importance of this lifelong task.

Be assured for counsel and guidance

on you I'll call and ask."

And so it was at heaven's door

as the angel prepared for flight

that God said, "Be good and do your best,"

and hugged His angel tight.

Heaven

With that, the angel grabbed a star

and tumbled from on high,

touching down as earth resounded

with a baby's sweet, pure cry.

On the chosen date of _____,

heaven's angel witnessed the birth

of _____,

God's newest blessing on earth.